Giant Snakes

The publisher wishes to thank Dr. James A. Oliver, Director Emeritus of the New York Zoological Society, for reading the text of this book.

For Michael, who loves giant snakes

Giant Snakes

(Original title: *Meet the Giant Snakes*)

by Seymour Simon

ILLUSTRATIONS BY HARRIETT SPRINGER

Random House/New York

Published in the United States by Random House, Inc., New York.

Library of Congress Catalog Card Number: 79-88704
ISBN: 0-394-62071-2

This edition published by arrangement with Walker Publishing Co., Inc.
(Originally published under the title *Meet the Giant Snakes*).

Manufactured in the United States of America
9 8 7 6 5 4 3 2 1 0
Random House Student Book Program Edition: First Printing, 1979

Contents

INDIAN PYTHON CONSTRICTING ITS PREY

Six Giants of the Snake World

Imagine a snake as long as a car. That's about the size of a boa constrictor. Now imagine a snake about as long as a big station wagon. That's about the size of an African python. Finally, imagine a snake about as long as a school bus. That's about the size of the biggest snakes of all, the anaconda and the reticulated python.

Two other giant-sized snakes are the Indian python and the amethystine python.

A dozen or so smaller kinds of pythons, the king cobra, and a few others are between 10 and 20 feet long. All the rest of the several thousand different kinds of snakes are under 10 feet long.

The giant snakes are found in just two families, the boas and the pythons. (The anaconda is a boa.) The two families are closely related. They look very much the same. The main difference is that all boas bear living young, while all pythons lay eggs. Another difference is that boas are found in the New World, mainly in South America and Central America. All pythons are found in the Old World, mainly in India, southeast Asia, and Africa.

ANACONDA SWIMMING

The giant snakes are the longest of living land animals. They are longer even than the elephant or the giraffe. The giant snakes are the lightest of the big animals. They have long, slender bodies. They use their flexible bodies to throw constricting coils around their prey.

The giant snakes cannot make any sounds other than a sort of hiss. They have no outside ears and probably cannot very well hear sounds carried in the air. They can, however, sense vibrations through the ground. The giant snakes can see fairly well, but mostly they sense the world through smell and through heat sensitive pits in the lower jaw. These senses help to locate prey animals at night.

Giant snakes move more silently and slowly than most other large land animals. They easily climb trees and crawl along branches.

Many giant snakes are also at home in the water. They can hold their breath for a long time underwater and swim with a sort of back-and-forth gliding motion. They can keep their eyes open underwater because they have clear, immovable watertight eye coverings. In fact, they are unable to close their eyes or blink.

AFRICAN ROCK PYTHON

Snakes depend upon sunlight, warm air, or a sun-warmed surface to keep warm. All the giant snakes live in warm places, in or close to the tropics. A snake becomes warm if the air around it is warm or it is resting on the warm ground or a warm rock. It becomes cold if everything around it is cold. For this reason, a snake is called a "cold-blooded" animal. A better name would be an *ectothermic* animal, meaning that it gets heat from its surroundings.

BOA CONSTRICTOR
WITH ITS YOUNG

The anaconda and boa constrictor give birth to fully formed young snakes. Two or three dozen young are born at a time. A newborn boa constrictor is about 1½ to 2 feet long. A newborn anaconda is about 2 to 3 feet long. Nobody knows just how often giant snakes lay eggs or have living young.

PYTHON INCUBATING EGGS

Most snakes pay no attention to their young, regardless of whether they lay eggs or bear them alive. But the giant pythons are very unusual. They lay as many as one hundred eggs at a time. Each egg is a bit larger than a chicken egg. The female python pushes the eggs into a pile. She coils her body around the eggs with her head resting on top. She remains like this until the eggs hatch. This may take as long as ten weeks. She will leave the eggs only rarely for a drink of water. The female python of some species raises her temperature when she is incubating her eggs. Every once in a while she shivers and muscular waves move up and down her body. Scientists think that these movements heat up her body and this warms the eggs.

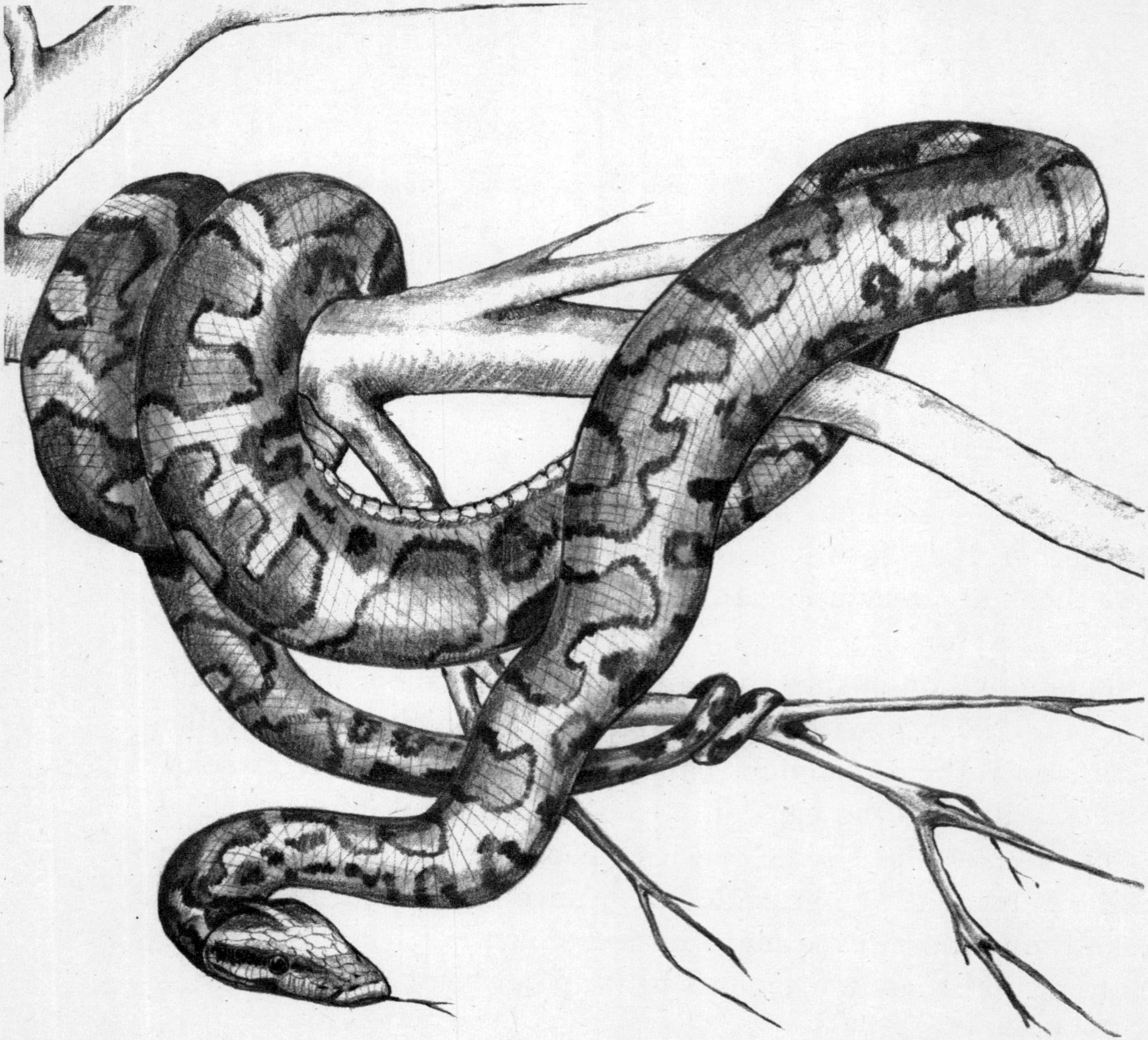

INDIAN PYTHON

Getting Food and Eating

How does a giant snake find food to eat? Many people have observed a python lying in wait on a tree branch or a rocky ledge on a jungle trail, and striking with open jaws at a passing animal. The python then coils around the animal and begins to squeeze.

Not all giant snakes wait for their prey. They also may hunt for prey. They search by crawling into cracks and burrows where animals may be hiding. Water living snakes go after fish, turtles, and young caimans.

Giant snakes can fast for a long time between feedings. Three or four good meals a *year* may be enough. There are many zoo records of giant snakes that did not eat for a year or longer without becoming ill.

All the giant snakes kill their prey by squeezing or constricting. First the snake grabs an animal with its teeth. Once it has a good hold, the snake wraps itself around the animal and the coils begin to squeeze hard.

ANACONDA DEVOURING A SMALL MAMMAL

Some people think that giant snakes crush their prey's bones to a pulp but that is not so. What happens is that the prey cannot breath and dies of suffocation. In a few minutes the animal is dead.

A snake can open its double-hinged jaws and elastic throat wide enough to swallow an animal much larger than the size of the snake's head. It may take a giant snake hours to swallow a really big meal. The time depends upon the prey's size and shape.

Almost any animal that is not too large may make a meal for a giant snake. It can eat rats, squirrels, lizards, birds, deer, antelopes, monkeys, jackals, and pigs. A giant snake may also feed on dogs, sheep, goats, chickens, and other domestic animals.

AFRICAN ROCK PYTHON AFTER A LARGE MEAL

Most of the animals eaten by giant snakes weigh less than 50 pounds. But there are rare reports of much larger animals being eaten. For example, one snake keeper fed an 80-pound pig to a 20-foot python. Another keeper fed an 84-pound goat to an even larger python. These records were topped by a keeper who fed his 24-foot python a pig weighing 120 pounds.

But the record large meal was eaten by an African python that measured 16 feet. This snake was found to have eaten a 130-pound impala (a kind of antelope). Because this snake was only 16 feet long, it is probable that a 25-foot snake could swallow an animal even larger.

ANACONDA COILED AROUND A BRANCH

Attacks on People

Giant snakes sometimes attack people but they almost never try to eat them. One reason is that most people are just too large for a giant snake. Another reason is that people are too smart to be caught easily by a giant snake. Still another reason is that people often stay together in groups and can help one another.

Most accounts of giant snakes attacking people are probably just made-up tales. Snakes usually avoid people. Those snakes that attack people are usually killed.

But some stories of attacks may be true. One of these stories came from an island in Indonesia. A scientist studying snakes told of a woman being swallowed by an 18-foot reticulated python.

Another story came from Burma. It seems that a salesman was on a hunting trip in the countryside. The salesman became the hunted instead of the hunter. He was reported to have been attacked and eaten by a 25-foot python.

There are other accounts of giant snakes attacking people but not of trying to swallow them. Usually the snake is hidden from view. Someone comes too close. The snake suddenly seizes the person in its jaws. The snake then tries to squeeze the person in its coils but a person is usually able to resist the attack.

Occasionally the snake continues to squeeze and will kill its victim. This story comes from an island in Lake Victoria in Africa. The snake was an African rock python, 14 feet long and nearly 1½ feet wide. The victim was a woman who had been washing clothes near a stream. A man came by and saw the clothes but no woman. He looked around and saw the woman in the snake's coils. He called for help. The python was killed but too late to save the woman.

Several stories of attacks on people by anacondas, the largest of the big snakes, come from South America. One story tells of a thirteen-year-old boy who disappeared while swimming in a river. His friends saw bubbles rising where the boy disappeared. One of them dived and was able to feel the body of a snake. They called for help, and a search began. After a day and a half of looking, the anaconda was found. It was quickly killed with a rifle. The boy's body was lying nearby.

It may seem to you that people are in great danger from giant snakes. But scientists and other people who handle snakes do not think so. They believe that many of the stories of attacks on people are either untrue or greatly exaggerated. It is more likely that a person will be hit by lightning than that he or she will be attacked by a giant snake.

If a giant snake does attack a person, it is probably because the snake mistakes the person for an animal that it normally eats. An attack on a person by a giant snake is news around the world. The fact that there are so few stories about snake attacks shows how rare they really are.

BABOONS ATTACKING A CONSTRICTOR

The Enemies of Giant Snakes

People are the worst enemies of giant snakes. Not only do people often kill any giant snake they see, but they sometimes hunt and kill snakes for their skins or meat or just to get rid of what they think are dangerous animals. Also as people build new cities, towns, and roads, there is less room for snakes to live and find the foods they need.

When giant snakes are small, they have many other enemies. Snake-eating birds, mammals, lizards, and even other snakes will eat a giant snake when it is only 2 or 3 feet long. But each foot added to a giant snake's length makes its enemy list grow shorter. By the time a snake is over 10 feet long, there are only a few animals that will attack it. When the snake is over 20 feet long, the list is very short.

Animals that hunt together may attack and kill giant snakes. One South American explorer described a herd of wild pigs attacking and eating a giant snake. A report from Africa tells of the same kind of attack on a giant snake by warthogs. A troop of baboons will also sometimes attack a giant snake.

There are some stories of crocodiles attacking and eating giant snakes. There are also reports of tigers and other large members of the cat family attacking snakes. Giant snake battles with animals such as elephants, bears, and sharks are either just made-up tales or may have been staged by people.

The Anaconda

The anaconda is found in the tropical parts of South America and also on the island of Trinidad. This muddy-green and black giant lives mostly in swamps and on the banks of lakes and slow-moving rivers. It hunts land animals such as deer, wild pigs, and large rodents. But it is a good swimmer and sometimes also eats water animals such as turtles, fish, or crocodiles. The anaconda mostly searches for its food at night.

If you take both length and bulk into account, the anaconda is the largest snake in the world. There are several reports of anacondas that measured over 30 feet long. A snake of almost record size was shot in a river by a team of oil explorers in eastern Columbia, South America, in 1944. After dragging the huge snake up onto the bank, the explorers measured its length with a tape ruler. It measured 37½ feet.

After measuring the snake the explorers went back to work. When they returned to skin the snake, they found that it had disappeared. It seems that the snake had recovered enough to crawl or swim away.

A Brazilian scientist examined many reports of giant snakes. He found one report of a snake killed in southern Brazil in 1913 that was measured by some Indians at just over 38 feet in length. After looking over all the reports on giant anacondas, the scientist decided that the biggest anacondas may be between 39 and 45 feet long. Despite all the reports of 30-foot anacondas, no living anaconda of over 25 feet has ever reached a zoo in the United States or Europe.

Not all scientists agree that anacondas can be that large. In the 1920s, Raymond L. Ditmars, at that time curator of reptiles of the Bronx Zoo, offered a one-thousand-dollar reward to anyone who could bring him an anaconda skin measuring over 40 feet long. No one ever claimed the reward. The largest skin sent to Dr. Ditmars was just over 21 feet long.

Trying to guess the size of a snake can be a tricky business. One scientist asked the members of an expedition to guess the length of an anaconda they had spotted. The guesses ranged all the way from 20 feet to 60 feet. When the snake was shot and measured with a tape ruler, it turned out to be only 19½ feet long.

Measuring the skins of snakes is even more difficult. James A. Oliver, a scientist who studied snakes, says that when a snake skin is removed, it is always stretched. In the case of giant snakes such as the anaconda, the stretched skin can be many feet longer than the living snake.

The most common method of measuring a living snake is to run a string along the snake's back and then measure the string. Even this method is not very accurate.

The anaconda is much thicker and heavier than other giant snakes that are the same length. For example, a 17-foot-long anaconda will probably weigh as much as a 24-foot-long python. You can see why the anaconda appears so much bigger than other giant snakes.

The Reticulated Python

The reticulated python has a beautiful pattern of skin colors. (The word *reticulated* means "covered with a network.") This giant snake has always been a favorite in zoos and circuses. In nature, the reticulated python is found in the hot, humid climates of southeast Asia and the Philippine Islands.

The reticulated python often lives and hunts near rivers and lakes. It is a good swimmer. Sometimes it even swims far out to sea. It is also a good climber. A few reports say that the reticulated python lives mostly in trees. At one time it lived in the middle of large cities in southeast Asia. Even as recently as 1970, a 24-foot reticulated python was run over and killed by a taxicab in a city in the Philippines.

It is strange to think of such a giant snake living in a city. But there are many reports of these pythons living in holes or cracks near buildings. At night they come out to hunt for chickens, ducks, cats and dogs.

Most adult reticulated pythons average over 20 feet in length. The longest reticulated python on record was found on the island of Celebes. After it was killed, the snake was carefully measured at 33 feet in length.

There are other reports of a 33-foot python killed in Java and a 30-foot one killed in Malaya. Several zoos in the United States have kept reticulated pythons that were over 28 feet long. Colossus, a reticulated python kept in Pittsburgh's Highland Park Zoo, was 28½ feet long and weighed 300 pounds. It died in 1966 at the ripe old age (for a snake) of thirty years.

Reticulated pythons seem to be among the biggest eaters of the snake world. One 25-foot python was fed two goats one day. A few days later it was fed an antelope. This totaled 138 pounds of food in less than a week! Can you imagine getting the food bill for a pet reticulated python?

The African Rock Python

The African rock python is third in size among the giant snakes. It is found all over Africa except in the great deserts. All the stories of giant African snakes come from meetings with this python because there are no other giant snakes found in Africa.

The African rock python lives in many different kinds of surroundings. It seems to be at home in grasslands, forests, farmlands, mountains, big lakes, swamps, and small rivers. It often climbs trees and hunts birds, monkeys, and other prey among the branches. It is a good swimmer and goes far from shore.

The African python is sometimes just called the rock python. This can be confusing, because the Indian python is sometimes also called the rock python. The African python is longer than the Indian python but has a thinner body.

The markings on an African rock python are dark brown against a light brown background. There are also specks of brown along its sides. Then entire skin looks very shiny under a bright light.

The largest rock python on record was found in West Africa. In 1932, a 32-foot-long one was shot in a flower hedge near a school. This giant python was much larger than the average. Most African rock pythons range from 13 to 20 feet.

The Indian Python

The Indian python has probably been seen in captivity by more people than any other giant snake. It looks much the same as an African rock python. It takes to handling more readily than any of the other large snakes and is a favorite in snake shows, in circuses, and carnivals.

The Indian python is found throughout the lowlands of India, Pakistan, Ceylon, and parts of China. In southeastern Asia, the Indian python lives in much the same areas as another giant snake, the reticulated python. Both of these pythons are at home in grasslands, occasionally climbing trees in forests, and swimming in the water. Both will eat almost any kind of animal that they can catch and swallow.

There have been no reliable reports of Indian pythons that were longer than 20 feet. The largest one on record was just over 19 feet long and weighed 200 pounds. There are many other records of Indian pythons that were between 18 and 19 feet. Many people think that there must be some 20-foot-long ones around.

Here is how one snake handler writes about how to handle an Indian python. He says that the snake will always wrap its body around you. But there is nothing to worry about, so long as the snake is not more than 12 or 13 feet. In other words, don't pick up any Indian pythons longer than 12 feet.

The Amethystine Python

Less is known about this python than about any of the giant snakes. It lives in Australia, New Guinea, and some of the nearby islands in the South Pacific. One collecting party in Australia found thirteen of these pythons in one day. They were found resting on rocks and in grassy areas along a riverbank.

Most places in the world have only one or two kinds of large snakes. Some places have none. But Australia and New Guinea have a dozen different kinds of pythons that are over 6 feet long. This is probably due to the fact that they have few enemies there and also have plenty of food.

The amethystine python has purple markings over a yellow-brown background. (An amethyst is a purple mineral.) This python is more slender than any of the other giants. The largest one on record was 28 feet long. Most are much smaller than that. The average is about 10 to 15 feet.

The amethystine python is often thought to eat kangaroos and wallabies. While the larger pythons probably do eat these animals when they can catch them, most of the amethystine python's food animals are much smaller. It often eats chickens and other domesticated animals.

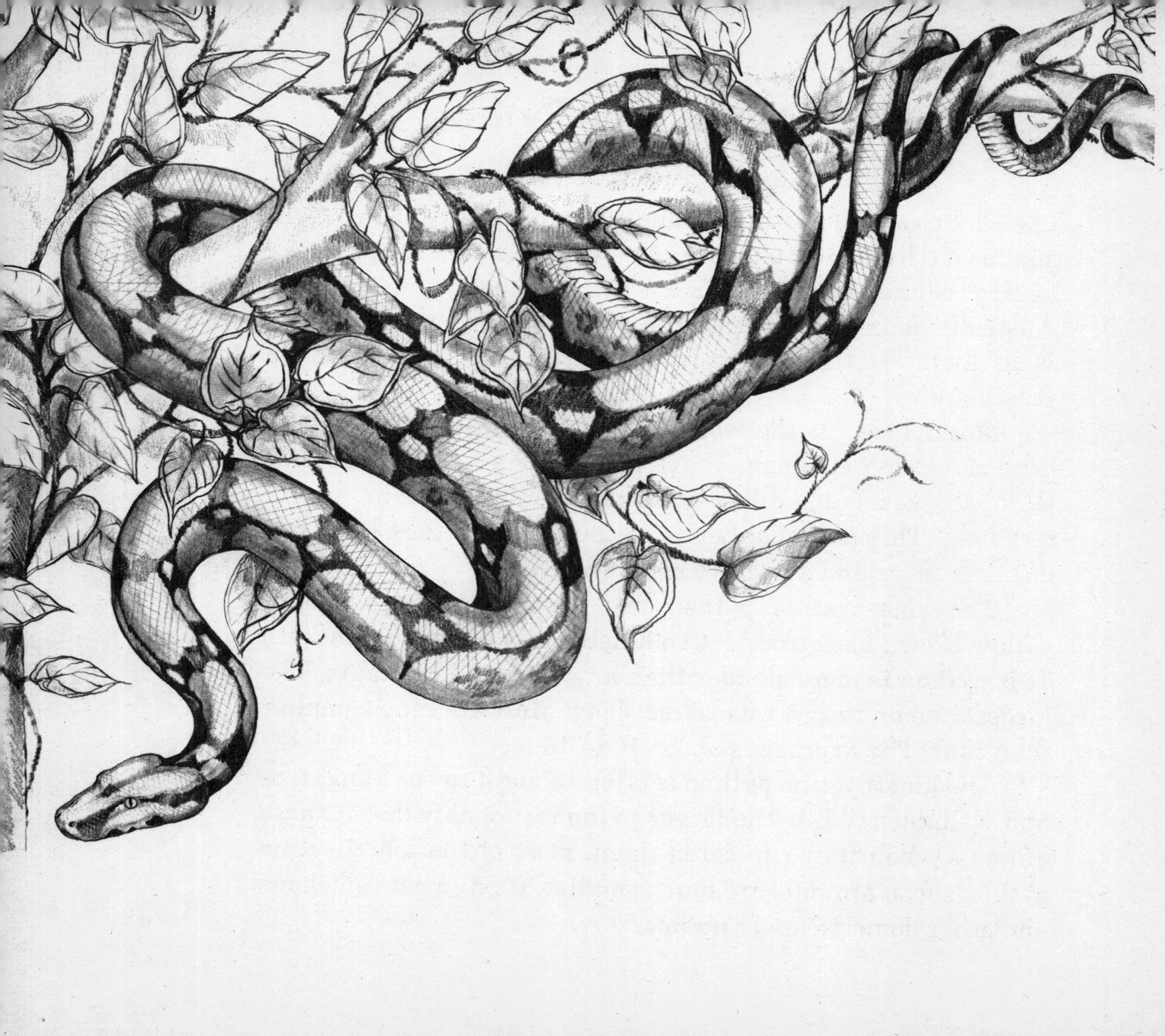

The Boa Constrictor

Many people think that the boa constrictor is the biggest of the giant snakes. They even call all large snakes boa constrictors. But actually boa constrictors are the smallest of the six giant snakes. And as we have seen, not all giant snakes are boa constrictors.

Boas are found from Mexico through much of South America. It's the only giant snake that you can find in nature within a day's car drive of the United States. Boas have been found just below some of the border towns of Texas and Arizona.

Boas have many different color patterns. The most beautiful kinds are in great demand as pets. These have chocolate-brown markings over a tan background. The markings often become reddish toward the tail. Most of the boas sold as pets are well under 10 feet long.

The largest boa constrictor on record was found on the island of Trinidad. It measured 18½ feet long just short of the 20-foot size that marks the real giant snakes. In South and Central America, the record is about 15 feet. In fact, any boa over 10 feet long is said to be exceptional.

Boas eat all kinds of small animals, such as lizards, birds, rats, squirrels, rabbits, and small wild pigs. They often raid chicken houses and will eat ducks, small dogs, and cats.

Boas make their homes in many different kinds of surroundings. They live in grasslands, planted fields, tropical forests, and even some deserts. While boas live in the same areas as anacondas, they do not live in the same kinds of spots. The anaconda is much more of a water-dwelling animal than the boa.

Small boas sometimes come into the United States as stowaways with banana shipments. A baby boa is about 1½ or 2 feet long. In a year it may double in length. In a few years it may grow to be 10 feet long. It's not a good idea to get a baby boa as a pet unless you are prepared to keep it when it is full grown. Keeping a pet boa in good health may be more of a task than you would like to undertake.

THE PA SNAKE IS ONLY A LEGEND

Legends and Tales of Giant Snakes

It seems that no matter what science tells us about snakes, many people still enjoy telling and hearing a good giant snake story.

An old Norse legend tells the story of the Midgard Snake, a child of Loki, the god of trickery and evil. Odin, the king of the gods, hurled the monster snake deep into the sea. But the Midgard Snake continued to grow and grow. Finally the snake grew so large that it encircled the entire world, holding its tail by its mouth.

Just a bit smaller was Yulungurr, the giant python in the legends of the Australian Bushmen. The python's long body stretched across the sky like a rainbow.

Still another legend of a giant snake comes from South America. It seems that a group of Indians were slowly making their way through a dense jungle. Suddenly they came upon a smooth wall too high to climb over. For two days they followed the path of the wall hoping to find an opening. Finally the wall ended in the head of a huge anaconda. The Indians fled before the sleeping giant snake might awaken and devour them.

Chinese writings tell the story of the giant Pa Snake, which was large enough to eat elephants. The Pa Snake was said to have taken three years to digest its meals, whereupon it ejected the elephant bones.

Two thousand years ago, the Roman army was fighting in North Africa. The reports of their battles tell of the capture of a snake 120 feet long. The monster snake was said to have killed several battalions of soldiers. The soldiers assaulted the snake with catapults loaded with heavy rocks. Finally the snake was overcome. Back in Rome, no one doubted the story. They awarded Regulus, the leader of the army, many honors for his great victory over the giant snake.

There are many tales and legends of giant snakes from all over the world. But it is sometimes difficult to tell the difference between a tall tale and a true story. For example, when Alexander the Great's soldiers fought their way through India, they probably saw many real giant snakes. But by the time the soldiers returned home, the snakes had become much larger. The soldiers told of snakes that had eyes as large as shields. They were supposed to be able to swallow oxen and deer at a single gulp.

Even in modern times there are stories and reports of giant snakes that are hard to believe.

In 1948, a newspaper in Brazil printed a far-fetched story of a giant anaconda 156 feet long. According to the story, the monster snake knocked down buildings and upset automobiles before it was finally killed by the army. Even today some people are taken in by such stories. Six years later still another snake story came out of Brazil, but this monster was only 120 feet long!

Giant snakes are like other animals, neither bad nor good. They act the way they must to eat and to live. They are parts of food webs that connect all living things. For example, the boa constrictor is very important in keeping down the numbers of rats and other rodents in parts of South and Central America. Killing off the boas would have a great effect on the natural life of these countries. Giant snakes help to maintain the balance of nature.